pillow pup

Dianne Ochiltree   illustrated by Mireille d'Allancé

Margaret K. McElderry Books
New York London Toronto Sydney Singapore

To Stella
— D. O.

My dog, Maggie,

is a pillow-pulling pup.

She pulls my pillow down

and chews my pillow up.

She takes it

and shakes it

from side to side,

On a tail-wagging,

floor-dragging,

zig-
zagging
ride.

Maggie bounces the pillow.

She pounces.

She prances.

She does one of her you-can't-catch-me dances.

Now off she goes!
It's a puppy chase.

Up and down the stairs we race.

Maggie shoots down the hall,

a doggie bullet.

I snatch my pillow back.

She tugs it.

I pull it.

Back and forth,

At last I grab my pillow
from her growling grin.

Maggie gives up.
She lets me win.

I put my pillow down.

She snatches it up and then . . .

Oh no, Maggie!

Here we go again!

Margaret K. McElderry Books
An imprint of Simon & Schuster
Children's Publishing Division
1230 Avenue of the Americas
New York, New York 10020
Text copyright © 2002 by
Dianne Ochiltree. Illustrations
copyright © 2002 by Mireille
d'Allancé. All rights reserved,
including the right of reproduction
in whole or in part in any form.
Book design by Kristin Smith
The text of this book was set
in Hobo. The illustrations are
rendered in pastels. Printed in
Hong Kong 10 9 8 7 6 5 4 3 2 1
Library of Congress Cataloging-
in-Publication Data: Ochiltree,
Dianne. Pillow pup / Dianne
Ochiltree ; illustrated by Mireille
d'Allancé.—1st ed.   p. cm.
Summary: A preschooler and
her dog have a pillow fight.
ISBN 0-689-83408-X [1. Dogs—
Fiction. 2. Play—Fiction. 3. Stories
in rhyme.] I. Allancé, Mireille d',
ill. II. Title. PZ8.3.O165 Pi 2002

FIRST
EDITION